UNICORN ACADEMY
...Where magic happens!

Rosa and Crystal

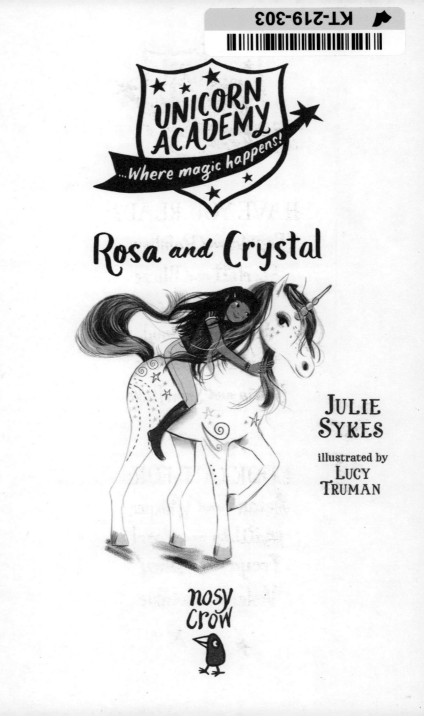

JULIE
SYKES

illustrated by
LUCY
TRUMAN

nosy
crow

To Fiona and Kirsty,
who make the magic happen.

First published in the UK in 2019 by Nosy Crow Ltd
The Crow's Nest, 14 Baden Place, Crosby Row
London, SE1 1YW, UK

Nosy Crow and associated logos are trademarks and/or registered
trademarks of Nosy Crow Ltd

A CIP catalogue record for this book will be available from the British Library.

Printed and bound in the UK by Clays Ltd, Elcograf S.p.A.

Papers used by Nosy Crow are made from wood grown in
sustainable forests.

ISBN: 978 1 78800 435 0

www.nosycrow.com

CHAPTER ONE

"Good work, Rosa. Crystal is the cleanest unicorn I've seen today and those silver ribbons look very pretty in her blue and purple mane and tail – a very good choice!"

"Thank you, Ms Rosemary." Rosa blushed, her heart swelling with pride. She'd been at Unicorn Academy for a month now and she had been worrying recently that she'd done something to upset Ms Rosemary, the Care of Unicorns teacher. Rosa loved being the best at things and, even though she always put her hand up first to answer questions or volunteer for jobs, for some reason Ms Rosemary had stopped picking her and kept asking the others instead. Rosa couldn't understand it.

"Well done," Crystal whispered, her warm breath tickling Rosa's face.

"Thanks!" Rosa stroked Crystal's sleek white neck, patterned with swirls of shimmery pink. Crystal was extremely pretty and Rosa had been thrilled when Ms Nettles, the head teacher, had paired them together on their first day at the academy. Crystal was always happy to go along with whatever Rosa wanted to do and they'd made friends immediately.

Ms Rosemary continued to inspect the other unicorns. The class was made up of the five girls from Diamond dorm – Rosa's dorm – as well as the students from Topaz and Ruby dorms.

"Whisper's mane is plaited perfectly, Ariana," Ms Rosemary said approvingly to the girl next to Rosa. Serious Ariana, who was always neat and tidy and whose clothes were spotlessly clean, looked very pleased.

"But, Matilda . . . oh dear!" Ms Rosemary shook her head as she inspected Pearl, Matilda's unicorn. The plaits in Pearl's mane were all different sizes, some of them were coming undone already and the tangle of different coloured ribbons in Pearl's tail looked as if they had been tied on at the very last minute. "What's happened here?" said Ms Rosemary, holding up Pearl's tail.

A few of the students giggled. Rosa cringed. She couldn't imagine anything worse than a teacher pointing out her mistakes in front of the whole class. Poor Matilda! But Matilda didn't look upset.

"Sorry, Miss," said Matilda, pulling a small sketchbook out from her pocket. "But I was just about to do Pearl's tail when I saw a robin land on the ribbon box. He was trying to pull out some ribbon and he looked so cute I just had to draw him. Look." She held out the picture. She had perfectly captured the little robin's cheeky expression.

Ms Rosemary seemed to soften slightly. "It's an excellent drawing but, Matilda, you are here at the academy to learn how to care for your unicorn and not to draw robins. You must try harder or you won't graduate at the end of the year. Do you understand?"

"Yes, Miss." Matilda pushed her tangle of red hair off her face and sighed. "It's just sometimes my fingers feel like they simply have to draw, but I'll try and stop them."

Ms Rosemary smiled and moved on.

"Shall we do something fun together when the grooming inspection's over?" Rosa whispered to Crystal.

"Ooh, yes! How about we go to the play park?" Crystal said, her ears pricking.

"Or we could go on the Safari Trail," said Rosa persuasively. "It goes all around the academy grounds. Apparently there are fox cubs, cave spiders and, if we're very lucky, we might even see a purple badger."

"OK, let's do that," said Crystal. "We can visit the play park another time."

"We could ask the rest of the dorm to come

with us too," said Rosa. She'd been really excited about making friends at the academy, but so far the others in her dorm had been quite reserved and quiet. The boys in Topaz dorm were often seen galloping around the grounds together, and the girls in Ruby dorm were usually in a big giggling group, but Diamond dorm weren't like that. They were all quite different and most of the time went off on their own.

Well, not any more, Rosa decided. *It's time we all had some fun together!*

Rosa waited for Ms Rosemary to finish her inspection and dismiss the class. Then she stood on an upturned bucket and clapped her hands together.

"Listen up, Diamond dorm! Crystal and I think we should all go on the Safari Trail together."

The four other girls from Diamond dorm stared at Rosa. She squared her shoulders and smiled

boldly back at her dorm-
mates even though her heart
was beating in double time.
Have confidence! That's what
Rosa's super-efficient mum
was always telling her. "It'll be
fun!" she declared.

"We'll come, won't we,
Twinkle?" said Violet, pushing
her dark plait over her shoulder.

"Definitely," whinnied Twinkle,
her unicorn.

Whisper nudged
Ariana eagerly.

"Whisper and I will
come too," Ariana said.

"And me and Pearl," said Matilda. She took off
her glasses to polish them and a pencil that had
been behind her ear fell to the ground. "So that's

where I put it!" she said, pouncing on it. "Look! I thought I'd lost it!" She beamed as she stood up with it.

The other girls all giggled, apart from Ariana, who just rolled her eyes. She was very well organised and didn't have much patience with scatter-brained Matilda.

Rosa felt very relieved that the others seemed to like her idea. She'd felt quite nervous about standing up in front of them all. "Freya?" she called, her confidence increasing. "What about you and Honey? You'll come too, won't you?"

Freya was staring intently at one of the automated trolleys that trundled around the stables, laden with sky berries for the unicorns to eat.

"Earth to Freya. Are you even listening to me?"

Freya jumped as Violet nudged her. "What's that?" she asked, looking round.

"Diamond dorm are going to ride the Safari Trail. Do you want to come with us?" Rosa repeated.

"No, thanks." Freya took out a tiny notebook from her pocket and began scribbling inside it.

"But you have to!" Rosa demanded, flushed by her success with the other girls. "We're all going. You have to come."

"Let's go with them – please, Freya!" begged Honey, Freya's unicorn.

"Sorry," said Freya, barely glancing up. "I'm too busy."

Honey looked very disappointed.

"We'll come with you. Jester and I love an outing. Where are we going?" Miki, a small boy with a cheeky smile, peered at Rosa through his long black fringe as he stopped on his way past them. His unicorn, a dainty creature with a shaggy dark blue mane and an exceptionally long tail, nodded enthusiastically.

"Thanks, Miki, but maybe another time? This outing is for Diamond dorm only. We're *all* going,"

said Rosa, looking pointedly at Freya. She jumped off the bucket. "Come along, everyone!" She led the way outside but, as everyone regrouped in the courtyard, Rosa noticed that Freya and Honey had stayed behind in the stables.

"Freya!" she shouted in exasperation.

"She's not coming," said Miki, cheerfully tagging along with the group. "How about Jester and I pretend to be Honey and Freya?" He mimed opening a notebook and frantically writing something inside it.

Everyone laughed, even Rosa, who couldn't help but feel frustrated with Freya. How would the girls in Diamond dorm ever become best friends like the girls in Ruby dorm if Freya kept refusing to do things with the rest of them?

"Sorry, Miki, but this is a Diamond dorm outing, and you're in Topaz. It has to be Freya and Honey. You and Jester can come next time," she said.

"OK then," Miki said. "Come on, Jester. Let's go and explore the gardens." He gave a dramatic sigh. "All on our own!"

Rosa felt bad, but she really wanted this to be a bonding experience for Diamond dorm.

"Freya . . ." Rosa began, looking pleadingly to the blonde-haired girl who had now come out.

"Nope," Freya said as she walked past, her plaits bouncing on her shoulders. "I told you — I'm busy. Stop being so bossy."

Rosa felt her face redden, but she quickly recovered when Violet sent her a friendly smile.

"Freya really is busy," Violet confided. "She told me the automated stable trolleys had given her an idea for something she wants to build. Something that moves! You know how much she loves anything to do with engineering."

Rosa frowned. She didn't care if Freya built a hundred moving things. How could going off on your own be as much fun as spending time with your dorm-mates and their unicorns? "We'll just

Rosa and Crystal

have to go without her then," she said, rather crossly. "The Safari Trail starts in the orchard near the river. That's where the red bills are supposed to be nesting. Get in line, everyone. Stay behind Crystal and me and don't forget to be quiet!"

Rosa and Crystal led the way through the apple trees to the stream at the bottom of the orchard.

It was one of many brightly coloured streams that criss-crossed Unicorn Island, carrying the magical waters that nourished the land. The multicoloured water came from the centre of the earth, right there in the grounds of Unicorn Academy. It flowed up through a glittery fountain and into Sparkle Lake, before starting on its journey around the island. Rosa almost had to pinch herself as she started towards the orchard. It was hard to believe she was really here, at Unicorn Academy, and training to be a guardian of Unicorn Island.

"I hope we do see a red bill," Rosa said to Crystal.

"We should do if we're quiet," Crystal reassured her.

Rosa loved wildlife and had always wanted to train to be an island guardian. It had been a dream come true when she received the letter inviting her to Unicorn Academy. Most pupils were at the academy for a year before they graduated. Some got to stay for longer if their unicorns needed more time to discover their magic power, or if they hadn't bonded with their unicorn. Rosa ran her fingers through Crystal's shimmery silken mane. Bonding was the highest form of friendship possible and Rosa would know that it had happened because a lock of her own straight black hair would turn the same shimmery purple as Crystal's mane. Rosa couldn't wait for that to happen!

"Red bills, two of them, and a chick, over there," hissed a voice, startling Rosa out of her thoughts.

In the middle of the stream, two red bills were fussing around a chick as it swam out of the reeds and splashed in the water. Rosa held her breath. The fluffy chick with its enormous crimson beak kept sneaking away from its parents to explore. Then the parents would chase after it, squawking with alarm, and herd it back. The second the red bill's parents saw the girls approaching they fled, hustling their chick into a reed bed and vanishing out of sight.

Rosa smiled at the sight and then turned to see who had spoken to her. "Miki!" she exclaimed, seeing the dark-haired boy. "What are you doing here? This is a Diamond dorm ride," she added accusingly.

"I told Miki he could come with us after all," Violet said quickly.

Rosa frowned. She was in charge of this expedition, not Violet.

"Sorry, Rosa," Violet rushed on. "But please let him stay. He knows a ton of stuff about the countryside. His parents keep a herd of reindeer in the north of the island. Miki spends a lot of

16

time watching the wildlife while he's minding the herd, don't you, Miki?"

Miki's brown eyes twinkled mischievously as he nodded. "You'd have missed the red bills if I hadn't pointed them out, Rosa."

Miki's smile was so infectious that Rosa couldn't help smiling back. "OK, you can stay," she agreed. "But no overtaking. This ride was my idea so I'm in charge!" She beamed happily. She loved being the leader! "Come on, everyone. We're going to have some fun!"

CHAPTER TWO

The Safari Trail was a huge success. Miki, Violet, Ariana and Matilda chattered all the way back, saying what a brilliant time they'd had. Rosa felt very content as they rode back to the stables. The only thing that bugged her was that Freya hadn't come too. How would Diamond dorm ever get to know each other and become friends if Freya kept refusing to join in? It wasn't fair on Honey, Freya's unicorn, either. She'd clearly wanted to come along.

Rosa felt very sorry for Honey as they arrived back in the stable block. She was standing dejectedly in her stable, all on her own. She whinnied to them as they clattered inside.

"Did you have a good time? What did you see? I want to know all about it! Oh, I wish Freya and I had come too!"

While Rosa brushed the dirt from Crystal's silky coat, Crystal told Honey all about the Trail ride. Honey hung on Crystal's every word.

"You should get Freya to join in more," Rosa told her.

"I do try," said Honey sadly. "But she won't listen."

When Rosa had settled Crystal with a large bucket of sky berries, she went inside. As she entered the academy buildings she noticed that the door to the Great Hall was open. The hall was one of Rosa's favourite rooms and she couldn't resist peeking inside. A ray of sunlight lit a path on the floor, drawing her in further. The hall had a domed roof that was made of coloured glass, and the rays of light shining through it made rainbow-coloured swirls on the floor. Rosa's eyes fell on the centre of the room, where the magical map stood. It was an exact replica of Unicorn Island in miniature, with tiny green valleys, golden beaches and secret forests. Rosa went closer.

"You've heard the news, then?"

"Freya!" Rosa hadn't heard the other girl coming up behind her. "What news?"

"Didn't you even notice the force field wasn't working?" Freya said. "Didn't you wonder why you could walk all the way up to the map?"

Rosa realised that the humming, glimmering force field that normally protected the map wasn't there any more. "I didn't," she admitted, cross with herself. She hated people being able to find fault with her. "So, what's the news?"

"The force field isn't working because the

magical map is broken. I just heard Ms Nettles telling Ms Willow, the new school nurse, about it. Ms Nettles thinks that Ms Primrose may have something to do with it. You've heard of Ms Primrose, right? The head teacher who was here last year."

"Everyone's heard of Ms Primrose!" said Rosa. Ms Primrose and an unknown friend had tried to take control of the island by harming Sparkle Lake and Unicorn Academy. "It can't be her, though. She was caught and she's been locked up. My dad says that she's so well guarded that she'll never be able to harm Unicorn Academy or the island ever again."

"Yes, but my mum told me that before Ms Primrose was captured she stole the model of Unicorn Academy from the map." Freya pointed to a gap next to Sparkle Lake, where a tiny replica of Unicorn Academy should have been. "And, just now, Ms Nettles told Ms Willow she thinks that's why the map is broken. The map can take you anywhere on the island, but you need the model of the school to get back. The map is clever. It wouldn't take you on an adventure unless it was certain that it could get you back safely. Watch this." Freya leaned in and, touching a stretch of beach on the West Coast, she said, "I want to go to the beach."

"Freya!" Rosa gasped in alarm. What if the map suddenly whisked Freya away? The teachers would be furious. No one was allowed to use the magical map without Ms Nettles' permission, not unless it was a dire emergency!

"See?" said Freya, her hand still touching the sand. "The map really is broken. I wish I could fix it."

"If all the staff can't fix it, what makes you think you could?" said Rosa.

Freya shrugged. "I'm good at fixing things."

"But it's a magical map," Rosa pointed out. "It will need magic to fix it." She heard a ringing. "There goes the dinner bell. We'd better hurry."

Freya was still staring intently at the map. Rosa tugged on her sleeve. "Come on, Freya. It makes all of Diamond dorm look bad if one person's late."

Freya shook her off. "When have I ever been

late? You really are bossy, you know."

Rosa stared after Freya as she stalked off. She didn't know what it was about her and Freya, but the two of them always seemed to end up irritating each other.

Dinner was eaten in the dining room. Diamond dorm sat at the table next to the tall windows that overlooked Sparkle Lake. Everyone was talking about the magical map.

"I can't believe it's stopped working," said Ariana, helping herself to hot garlic bread, oozing with butter, from a basket on the table. "What if we need to get somewhere on the island quickly?"

Worry niggled in Rosa's tummy as she chased a strand of spaghetti around her plate. The map was important to the island's guardians, who needed to be able to react quickly if there was a problem on the island that required their help. What if something serious happened and no one could get there in time to sort it out?

"If the reason for the map not working is that Ms Primrose stole the model of the school, then Ms Nettles should make her give it back," said Rosa.

"Maybe Ms Primrose doesn't have it any more. Maybe she lost it," said Matilda.

"Like you would," Ariana muttered, with a swish of her braids.

Matilda grinned, not at all put out. "Yep!"

"Maybe she hid it," Violet suggested.

Rosa's eyes widened. "She might have done. It might even be somewhere here in the academy. We could try and find it. Think how thrilled Ms Nettles would be if Diamond dorm got the map working again. All the teachers would be so pleased with us. Who wants to help me look?"

"I'm in," said Violet, eagerly.

"Me too," said Ariana, and Matilda nodded.

"We could start by searching Ms Primrose's old study," said Rosa, her mind whirling. "There might be a clue there. Eat up, everyone, and no asking for seconds. We've got important work to do."

The girls ate quickly, except for Freya, who kept stopping to write things in her notebook.

"Are you nearly done?" Rosa asked her as everyone else stood up to leave.

"No," said Freya, not even looking up as she somehow managed to eat ice cream with one hand while sketching out a complicated-looking diagram with the other. "But you lot go on. I'm not coming."

"What a surprise!" said Rosa, annoyed. But Freya didn't seem bothered by her tone. She just carried on sketching.

"Come on," Rosa said, turning to the others. "We'll see if *we* can find the model, because *we*

Rosa and Crystal

care about the academy."

She stomped away from the table. Violet hurried alongside her. "Freya does care too," she said. "She just doesn't always like joining in."

"Hmm," said Rosa, raising her eyebrows in disbelief.

She led the others up the stairs towards the teachers' rooms. Rosa didn't know exactly where Ms Primrose's old study was, but surely it couldn't be that hard to find, could it?

"Do you know where we're going?" Ariana asked as Rosa led them along the twisty corridors. "Only I'm sure we've passed that clock engraved with unicorns twice already."

"That was a different clock," Rosa lied. To her relief she suddenly caught sight of a door that had a faded nameplate on it saying *"Ms Primrose"*. "Look, we're here now. I told you I knew the way!"

Rosa pressed her ear to the dark wooden door

and listened. The room sounded empty, just as she would have expected, but she knocked anyway, just to be sure. Then she opened the door cautiously. The study appeared not to have been touched since Ms Primrose left. The walls were lined with bookcases and pictures of unicorns.

There was a large desk with pens spread over it, and a pile of books and papers. Behind the desk there was a picture of a rearing unicorn, its head surrounded by a glowing mane and its haunches covered in a starry pattern. The chair was shoved back as if Ms Primrose had just been called away for a minute. It made Rosa feel uneasy, but she pushed the feeling away. She was in charge – she had to seem confident!

"Everyone spread out," she whispered. "Remember, we're looking for a tiny model of the school."

"Look everywhere," Ariana added, her brown eyes serious. "It might be hidden in a secret drawer or cupboard."

"That's exactly what I was going to say!" Rosa set to work at once, emptying the drawers of the large desk. She was disappointed not to find anything other than stationery, pens and fluff in any of the drawers. Rosa tapped the bottom of each one in the hope of finding a hidden compartment.

"Matilda!" hissed Ariana, who was taking

books from a shelf and stacking them on the floor in neat piles as she worked her way along. "Don't dump those papers over here. You're messing up my system."

"Sorry!" Matilda pushed her red hair out of her eyes, leaving a smear of dust on her cheek. "Isn't this fun? Ooh, look at those glittery pencils. I'd love a set like that." She brushed past the pile of books as she hurried towards a set of silver and gold pencils lying on one of the shelves.

"Stop!" squeaked Ariana as a tower of books toppled over with a crash, taking a second tower down with it. "Oh, Matilda!"

"It's not as bad as it looks." Violet quickly dropped to her knees and began helping Ariana to pick up the scattered books and papers.

Rosa came over to help. As she picked up a book, something small and silver fell out of it and landed on the floor with a clink. "What's that?"

"A key," said Violet, seizing it. "It's so tiny. I wonder what it's for."

Rosa took the key. It was slender, with a rearing unicorn at one end. The part that went in the lock was pointed and looked like a star. The rearing unicorn seemed familiar.

Rosa tapped the key in the palm of her hand as she tried to remember where she'd seen it before.

"That's it!" Her eyes fell on the picture hanging behind Ms Primrose's desk. It was of a unicorn with a mane that looked like a halo. Excitement shivered in her tummy. "The picture and the key, they're the same!"

Rosa crossed the room. She wasn't sure what she was looking for, but she was certain the key and the picture were linked.

"Look at the stars!" she exclaimed.

The unicorn in the picture had a cluster of stars on its haunches identical in shape to the end of the key. Rosa squinted at them and then she noticed that one had a small hole. She held the key up to the star and it slipped inside. "It's a lock," she gasped.

The others crowded round as the key turned with a soft click and the painting swung slowly away from the wall, revealing a golden safe.

CHAPTER THREE

"Look at that!" Rosa stared at the hidden safe. She could hardly breathe she was so excited. Maybe they were about to find the model of the school!

"I bet it's locked," said Violet.

Rosa turned the dial. To her surprise, the lock opened immediately.

"Be careful," warned Ariana as Rosa opened the door and reached inside.

To Rosa's disappointment, there was no little model of the school inside the safe, just a large rolled-up piece of paper tied with a gold ribbon. "There's a scroll," she said, pulling it out.

Curiously, she undid the bow and went to the desk. She spread the map out, anchoring the ends with two photo frames to stop them from curling back up.

Everyone crowded around.

"It's a map of somewhere called the Glittering Cavern!" said Violet, pointing to a label.

"It's hand-drawn and very good," said Matilda appreciatively.

The map, neatly drawn in sparkling rainbow inks, showed an incredible ice cavern full of multicoloured icicles and surrounded by a complicated maze of frozen passages.

"Look at those stalactites and stalagmites," breathed Rosa. "Did you ever see anything so beautiful?"

"Or dangerous," added Ariana, with a shiver. "Imagine if one of those stalactites snapped. It could spear you if you were standing underneath it!"

"See that?" Rosa made an excited stab at a tiny picture of a building marked with a cross, right in the centre of the cavern. "It's Unicorn Academy."

"What does it mean?" wondered Violet. "Why

would there be a drawing of the academy inside an ice cave?"

"Perhaps Ms Primrose was planning on destroying the academy by freezing it in ice," said Matilda, her green eyes huge behind her glasses.

Rosa frowned. "Why would she do that?"

Matilda had pulled a pencil from one of her pockets. She chewed the end thoughtfully. "Um. . . Well, everyone said Ms Primrose wanted more power. She did lots of terrible things before she was caught. Maybe that's why?"

But a better idea was growing inside Rosa. "No, do you know what I think? I think this is more like a treasure map and it marks the spot where Ms Primrose hid the model of the school! That's why the academy is so tiny. It's not the actual school — it's the model!"

"Ooh yes!" said Violet. "I bet you're right." Excitement fizzed through Rosa. "Imagine if we followed this map and found it? Once the model is returned, the magical map will work again and everyone will be so pleased with us!" She could hardly get the words out in her excitement. "Let's go to this Glittering Cavern and bring the model home!"

Ariana frowned. "It would be far more sensible to just give the map to Ms Rosemary or Ms Nettles. They'll know what to do with it and be able to go there and get the model."

"But think how much more fun we could have solving the mystery ourselves," said Rosa. "We could ask our unicorns to come with us. It would be a real adventure."

Matilda nodded. "It really would."

But Ariana shook her head. "It could be really dangerous."

"We don't need to decide right now," Violet said quickly. "Let's go back to the dorm." She glanced around and shivered uneasily. "I keep feeling like someone is watching us!"

"OK," said Rosa. "We can carry on talking in our lounge, where no one can hear us."

Rosa replaced the key in the book then, hiding the map under her thick school hoodie, she led the girls out. Luckily they didn't meet anyone until they were near their dorm. As they rounded a corner, they saw Freya hurrying down the corridor ahead of them.

"Freya!" Rosa called. "Wait up! We're going to our lounge. We've got something *really* important to discuss. Come with us!"

But Freya just disappeared around the corner. Disappointed, Rosa led the other girls to the Diamond dorm lounge. A fire was burning in the hearth.

"I've got a bag of marshmallows somewhere," said Matilda. "Let's toast them."

Rosa and Crystal

While Matilda searched in her locker for the sweets, Rosa watched the leaping flames in the fireplace. The more she thought about her idea, the more sense it made. Ms Primrose must have hidden the model in the Glittering Cavern. Why else would she have marked the map with a picture of the school and a cross and then hidden the map in a safe? They had to find it!

Matilda appeared waving a fat bag of pink and white marshmallows and a bundle of toasting forks. "Here we go!"

"Matilda, watch out!" said Ariana, ducking as Matilda almost poked her with the forks. "Here, let me give them out. No, not that one – that's your pencil!"

The girls giggled as Ariana removed a pencil from the middle of the toasting forks and gave it back to Matilda. She handed out the forks. "Remember, don't get too close to the fire when you toast the marshmallows," she warned everyone.

"OK, so about the map," Rosa started as Violet passed around the marshmallows. "I've been thinking—"

"I'm not going," Ariana interrupted firmly, kneeling down by the fire. "I really think we have to tell the teachers."

"But that's boring!" Rosa protested.

"Look, it's too late to do anything now," Violet said. "Why don't we sleep on it and decide in the morning?"

Matilda and Ariana were already leaning forward and holding their marshmallows over the flames.

"All right," sighed Rosa. Squeezing between Matilda and Ariana, she banged her toasting fork down on the edge of the hearth. "OK, everyone. I've decided we won't do anything with the map until tomorrow. Until then, it's going to be a Diamond dorm secret. You are not to tell *anyone*," she added, giving them all an extra hard stare. "Is that understood?"

"Ooh, I do love a secret," said Matilda. "My big brother told me an amazing secret just before I left home to come here. If you promise not to tell—"

"Matilda!" Rosa interrupted. "A secret is only a secret if you don't tell anyone!"

Matilda turned pink. "I know," she said, with a guilty smile. "But none of you know my brother, so it won't matter if—"

"It does matter," said Rosa firmly, her gaze switching from Matilda to Ariana, who she thought was definitely the most likely to go and tell a teacher. "This map is Diamond dorm's secret. If anyone talks about it, especially to a teacher, then you'll have me to deal with!"

Matilda gave a squeak. "Scary!"

Rosa's fingers trembled as she pushed a marshmallow on to the end of her toasting fork. She was pleased how fierce she'd sounded even though she'd felt anything but fierce inside. Violet was right, though. It was too late to do anything with the map now. But tomorrow was Saturday and that meant they didn't have any lessons to go to. As soon as she had persuaded the others to do what she wanted, they could try and think up a way of getting to the Glittering Cavern. Though first Rosa had another problem to solve. *Where* exactly on Unicorn Island was the Glittering Cavern? She didn't have a clue!

CHAPTER FOUR

Rosa was up early the next morning, waking everyone up. "Today we're going to look for the Glittering Cavern!"

"Go away. I'm a bear. I'm hibernating," groaned Matilda, burrowing deep inside her pink and silver duvet.

But Rosa wouldn't leave Matilda alone. She tickled her until she finally sat up, groping for her glasses, while Rosa flung the curtains wide, flooding the room with winter sunlight.

Rosa had loved Diamond dorm from the moment she'd first set eyes on it. It was a tower

"Whoops!" she giggled.

Ariana sighed.

At last everyone was ready, but as they walked to the stables Rosa fell behind the others and slipped inside the hall to look at the magical map once more. It seemed so forlorn without the buzz of the magical force field. The hole where the academy should have been was like a missing tooth. Rosa reached out hesitantly and touched the map.

"Show me where the Glittering Cavern is," she breathed. "Please," she added hopefully. A tremble ran through her fingers. Rosa snatched her hand away. Was the map trying to work? What if it managed to take her to the Glittering Cavern? Without the model of the school to bring her back, she might be stuck there for good. Rosa pushed her straight, dark hair behind her ears and bent to study the map again. The gap where the academy should have been was glowing.

I think the map's asking for my help, Rosa thought suddenly. *I think it wants me to find the model of Unicorn Academy.*

"I will help you," she whispered. "Just show me where the Glittering Cavern is."

Another area of the map suddenly began to glow. It was a ridge of snowy mountains to the north of the academy. Rosa caught her breath. Was that where the Glittering Cavern was? The mountains looked like just the kind of place where an icy cavern might be found.

The glow faded away and Rosa was filled with a warm sense of duty and pride. The map had chosen *her* to help! *Well, I'm not going to let it down,* she thought.

She ran full pelt to the stables, hoping to catch the others up before she got there. But the rest of Diamond dorm were already there and Rosa heard their cheers and shouts of laughter as she opened the stable door. A stream of bubbles drifted out, floating past her and into the sky. There was another loud cheer. Whatever was going on?

Rosa burst inside. The rich smell of burnt sugar hung in the air. Rosa immediately recognised the smell. *Magic!* Her mother's unicorn, Ace, was a fire unicorn and whenever he did magic the air smelled just the same. She saw a crowd of people gathered around Jester's stable.

"Jester's found his magic," said Violet, budging up to let Rosa in. "He's got bubble magic. It's the coolest thing ever. And Miki and Jester have just bonded – look at Miki's hair."

Rosa couldn't take her eyes off Miki. He was standing in the centre of an enormous silvery bubble that wobbled and shimmered around him, so at first she didn't notice his hair. But there it was, a streak of dark blue that was just noticeable against his own black locks.

"Do it again," Matilda was begging. "Please, Miki, do the bubble walk again. I want to sketch you."

"All right," said Miki. He placed his hands against the walls of the bubble. Then, pushing gently against it, he took a careful step forward. The bubble quivered. Rosa held her breath – was it going to burst? Miki pushed against the shimmering wall and the bubble suddenly tipped forward, rolling like a giant ball. Miki kept going, walking slowly, an enormous grin plastered on his face. As his confidence increased, he walked faster, rolling along the walkway until the bubble hit a broom propped against the wall. With a loud pop, it burst on the bristles, sending thousands of tiny bubbles drifting up into the air. Miki leapt onto Jester's back and they took a bow.

Everyone clapped and cheered. "I can't wait

to tell Mum and Dad," said Miki breathlessly. "Bubble magic is awesome. When Jester has practised his magic more, he'll be able to make really strong bubbles. We can use them to protect the reindeer from wolves when we move them from their winter pastures to the summer ones."

Rosa clapped along with the other students even though she felt a bit jealous. Why hadn't she and Crystal bonded? They'd been friends from the moment they set eyes on each other. Rosa was also desperate to know what magic Crystal would have.

"Hurry up, Diamond dorm," she said. "We need to talk!"

"Can't we stay here a bit longer?" said Violet. "Jester's going to try and build a bubble bridge next."

"Great," whispered Rosa, rolling her eyes at Violet. "Let me know when he's finished. Then he can make a bubble road that leads to the Glittering Cavern, because that's where we need to go instead of hanging around here in the stables! Come on, everyone," she ordered sharply. "There isn't time for this. We seriously haven't got a second to waste!"

CHAPTER FIVE

"So, what do you think?" Rosa looked at everyone. They were all standing in a group outside the stables with their unicorns. She had even managed to pique Freya's curiosity enough to make her join them with Honey. "I'm sure the magic map gave me a definite sign that we should go to the Glittering Cavern. It's in some mountains that are not too far away. We could ride there in about four hours I think. We could be back by dinner if we leave soon."

"I think we should go," said Violet. Twinkle nodded.

"I still think it's too dangerous," protested Ariana. "And it's a really long way."

"Please let's go," said Whisper, her unicorn. "It sounds really exciting."

"We'll have a vote," decided Rosa. "All those in favour of going to the Glittering Cavern today, raise your hands or nod your heads."

All the unicorns nodded enthusiastically and all the girls, apart from Ariana and Freya, raised their hands. Freya hesitated for a moment and then nodded and raised her hand too. Honey whinnied in delight.

"It's decided then!" Rosa exclaimed. "We've voted and it's agreed. We're all going to try to find the Glittering Cavern – and the missing model of the academy."

"All right," said Ariana reluctantly. "But we must be careful, and what will we do about food?"

"I'll deal with that," Rosa declared. "Meet me

back here in an hour and we'll set off then!" She was thrilled. Finally Diamond dorm were going to do something all together, and just imagine how pleased the teachers would be if they came home with the missing model!

"You're the best, Rosa," Crystal said, nuzzling her as the others went off to get breakfast. "I love the way you organise everyone."

Rosa hugged her. "We'll find the model," she told her.

"I know we will!"

★

Rosa arranged for Cook to give everyone a packed lunch and gathered together some blankets, packing them into a rucksack with some rope and a compass.

At last they all set off, riding their unicorns northwards, keeping on course with the help of Rosa's compass. All the unicorns seemed very excited to be riding out on an adventure. Rosa kept noticing a flurry of pink sparks swirling around Crystal's hooves as she trotted along. The February day was sunny and cold, but Rosa, in the lead, went at such a fast pace that it wasn't long before Crystal was thirsty.

"I need a drink," she declared, changing course and trotting towards a babbling brook at the far end of the meadow they were riding through.

"Water!" squealed Pearl, splashing straight into

it with Matilda still on her back.

Rosa, Freya, Ariana and Violet dismounted. Freya let Honey take a long drink while she stood with a faraway look on her face.

I bet she's thinking about making some sort of machine, thought Rosa, with a flicker of irritation. *Why can't she just focus on what we're doing now?*

Crystal finished drinking and shook her head, spraying everyone with rainbow-coloured water droplets.

"Eeew!" screamed Matilda, getting splashed. "Water fight!"

"Yay! Water fight!" Pearl stamped her hooves in the brook.

Whisper retaliated, creating a mini whirlpool with his hooves as he kicked up the water.

"Stop!" cried Ariana desperately. "Please stop. Whisper, you're soaked. How can I ride you when you're that wet?"

Whisper was having too much fun to listen.

He stamped a hoof, sending a wave of coloured water cascading over Twinkle and Honey, and an even bigger wave over Crystal.

"Take that!" whinnied Crystal. Pink sparks swirled around her as she stamped in the brook, over and over again.

Rosa's nose wrinkled as she caught a whiff of something sweet in the air. "Crystal!" she gasped. "Look at you!"

For a second, Crystal was lost in a whirl of snowflakes that spun around her in a sparkling white mist. The unicorns stopped splashing and stared, their mouths hanging open in wonder. Gradually the snowflakes stopped spinning and melted away.

"That was awesome!" Pearl exclaimed. "Do it again."

Crystal seemed dazed. "W. . . W. . . What just happened?" she stuttered.

"You made it snow," said Honey, staring at Crystal's hooves. "I think you must have got your magic!"

"Did I?" Crystal lifted a hoof, holding it awkwardly as if it didn't belong to her. "I was just thinking how cold the water was and that it reminded me of snow."

"Do it again," urged Rosa.

Crystal concentrated hard and smacked her hoof into the brook. Snowflakes spun around like a mini whirlwind then danced along the surface of the water.

"Oh, Crystal," said Rosa, her breath catching. "You've definitely got your magic."

"Snow magic!" Crystal exclaimed, rearing up with her mane and tail streaming behind her. "Just the same as my grandma. I can't wait to tell her. This is my best day ever."

Matilda and Violet clapped and cheered as

Crystal cantered out of the water and Rosa threw her arms around her neck. Her unicorn had found her magic! The first of the unicorns in Diamond dorm! She felt like she was going to burst with pride. She sneaked a look at her hair. Had they bonded too, like Miki and Jester had? Her heart sank when she saw there was no coloured streak in her hair. *Never mind.* Rosa shook off her disappointment. She was sure it would happen soon.

"You know what else I can do with snow magic?" Crystal said to Rosa.

"Er, build a snowman?" Rosa asked.

Crystal puffed out her chest. "No, silly, I can make a snow twister! It's a special kind of whirlwind made from magical snow that doesn't feel cold at all – in fact it's lovely and warm. A snow twister can be used to move things from one place to another. I bet I can make a snow twister

Rosa and Crystal

that will take us all to the Glittering Cavern!"

"Really?" Rosa gasped.

Crystal nodded. "Gather round. It's easier if we all stand close together."

"Are you sure this is safe?" asked Ariana.

"Perfectly! I've ridden in Grandma's snow twisters and it's totally safe." Crystal fell silent as she concentrated on using her magic. Rosa laid a hand on her mane for encouragement as Crystal stomped on the grass with her hoof. "Take us to the Glittering Cavern!" she whinnied.

Pink sparks flared up then died away. Everyone looked at each other.

"Try again," urged Rosa. "You can do this, Crystal. You're the best unicorn in the world."

Tossing her mane in delight, Crystal banged on the ground again. This time, sparks crackled around her, twirling into the air as a pink snow twister curled from under her feet and began to

63

whirl in a tight circle around the girls and their unicorns. A dark curtain of silky hair blew over Rosa's face then her tummy swooshed as the snow twister swept her from her feet and twirled her high into the air.

"We're off to the Glittering Cavern!" she cried.

CHAPTER SIX

Rosa clung on to Crystal's mane, pink snowflakes spinning around her as the twister carried them all away. She was surprised how warm she felt. The snowflakes whirling around her face and catching in her hair were soft and cosy, like a fleecy blanket. All too soon, the twister slowed as it began to descend. The snowflakes shimmered and turned transparent and then Rosa hit the ground with a jolt, tipping forward and landing on her knees.

"Whoops! Sorry about that," panted Crystal.

Rosa got to her feet and clutched hold of

Crystal, her legs feeling wobbly. "I think I might need to work on landings," gasped Crystal.

The others were picking themselves up beside Rosa. In front of them was a snowy mountain range. The ground they were standing on was frozen solid, covered with frost.

"We're really here," said Freya. "That was such cool magic, Crystal." She frowned. "Are you OK?"

Rosa looked at Crystal, whose sides were heaving. "You do look exhausted," she said in concern.

"It was hard work," Crystal panted. "But I'll be fine in a bit."

While Crystal got her breath back, Rosa and the others gazed around.

"Look at that giant cave," said Violet, pointing. "Do you think that's the entrance to the maze?"

Matilda went over and peered inside. "There

are lots of those long icicle things in here," she called. Pulling out her sketchpad, she started to draw.

The others joined her. The cave was enormous, with a high domed roof, silvery-white stalagmites twisting up from the floor and pointed stalactites hanging from the icy ceiling, which glowed a silvery blue. Three tunnels led out of the cave. Rosa shivered into her hoodie as she pulled out the scroll taken from Ms Primrose's study. "This must be *this* entrance here," she said, spreading the map on a nearby boulder and stabbing her finger at one edge of the drawing. "To get to the middle, we need to take the third tunnel."

Rosa went to roll up the map, but Freya stopped her.

"Wait, the picture doesn't match these tunnels. On the map, the passages twist away, but these tunnels –" Freya pointed ahead of her – "don't seem to twist at all. They each go in a straight line. I think we're at this entrance here," she continued, placing a finger on the opposite side of the map. "Which means we should probably follow the second tunnel."

"No, no, no. You're wrong," Rosa insisted. "The tunnels might start off straight, but I bet they then begin to twist."

Freya went over to the tunnels to investigate.

Crystal nudged Rosa with her nose. "Rosa, maybe you should listen to Freya," she said softly.

Rosa was surprised. Crystal never told her what she should do. "But I'm sure I'm right," she whispered.

"Rosa, these tunnels really do go straight into the mountain for quite a long way before they start to twist," said Freya, looking back over her shoulder. "That's not what the map shows."

Rosa realised everyone was looking at her

expectantly. She couldn't back down. "It's a hand-drawn map. It's not going to be that accurate," she said. "I'm good at map-reading so just trust me."

"Last week Ariana came top in the map quiz Ms Rivers gave us in Geography and Culture," Freya said. "Perhaps she should look at the map and see what she—"

"No!" interrupted Rosa forcefully. "I'm in charge of this adventure and I say we go down this tunnel."

Crystal nudged her arm as if she wanted to say something, but Rosa ignored her. "This way, everyone!"

She vaulted on to Crystal and set off. Matilda and Violet shrugged and followed on their unicorns.

Rosa glanced back. Ariana and Freya were deep in conversation at the tunnel's entrance. "Hurry up or you'll get left behind," she shouted.

Ariana and Freya exchanged a look before joining her with their unicorns. But the argument had left an awkward feeling in the air and now they all rode in silence.

After a while, Rosa's teeth began to chatter. "If only the passage was as cosy and warm as your snow twister," she whispered to Crystal. "I wish we could go faster."

"The path is too icy," said Crystal as she carefully picked her way around the weirdly shaped stalagmites. "If we go faster, we'll start to slip and fall." She pulled up suddenly as the path split, one way rising up and the other sloping down. "Which way now?"

"That's easy," said Rosa. "The cavern is in the middle of the map and underground so we have to go west, which is left."

"How do you know which side of the cavern we are?" called Freya. "We might be the other side, in which case we need to go east."

"I just know," said Rosa, exasperated.

"But you might be wrong," Freya pointed out.

"Fine, I'll show you the compass," sighed Rosa, wishing Freya didn't always have to argue with her. She pulled out her compass. "Oh, that's weird. The needle won't stay still."

"That is odd," said Violet. "The compass

should work underground."

Ariana looked uneasy. "Magic can make compasses behave strangely. What if it's gone all crazy because of something magical? What if we're walking into a trap?"

Rosa laughed. "A trap? Why would Ms Primrose leave a trap for herself? No, I think the compass must just have been damaged in the snow twister."

"But how could a snow twister damage it?" asked Freya.

Rosa didn't know, but she couldn't admit that. "I must have sat on it when we landed," she lied. "Come along. If we go down here, I'm sure we will reach the cavern soon."

"Rosa. . ." Crystal began.

"It's OK, Crystal. I know I'm right," said Rosa, trying to sound confident.

But after continuing on for a very long time, riding through caverns and splashing through a stream, the tunnel they were in grew narrower and the ceiling lower so that the girls had to lie over their unicorn's necks to avoid bumping their heads. At the back, Ariana and Freya started whispering together again.

Let them whisper, thought Rosa. They'd soon be thanking her when they reached the Glittering

Cavern at the centre of the ice maze. According to the map, they were almost there.

"Hurry," she whispered to Crystal. Rosa imagined how amazing it would be if they returned to school with the model. Suddenly a noise startled her out of her thoughts. It started like the rustle of wind through leaves, but it quickly grew to a roar. The tunnel turned even colder as the roaring noise came bowling towards Crystal and Rosa.

"W. . . What is it?" whinnied Crystal, stopping dead.

"I don't know. I—" Rosa broke off with a yell as a squeaking, whirring cloud of creatures came flying around the corner, filling the tunnel. Rosa felt icy cold as the black mass buzzed over and around her, wings snagging in her hair and tickling her ears. The air rang with high-pitched squeaks.

"What are they?" she yelled, batting the creatures away while shielding her head with her other hand.

"Ice bats!" Twinkle whinnied from behind them. "We must have disturbed their roost!"

Crystal and the other unicorns hopped from side to side in a futile attempt to avoid the icy creatures.

"Everyone stay still," called Violet from the back. "The ice bats won't hurt us."

"They're sooo cold," gasped Ariana, her teeth chattering loudly.

As the stragglers passed over, the air grew warmer and the unicorns stopped leaping around. Rosa stroked Crystal's trembling neck. "It's OK," she soothed. "We can go on now."

"Those poor ice bats," said Crystal guiltily. "We scared them away." She continued around the corner. "Look," she said as the tunnel ended in an icy wall covered with jutting-out ledges. "This must be where they were roosting."

Rosa stared at the frosty wall ahead. They'd come to a dead end. She reached out and pushed on it with her hand as if it might suddenly melt away. "Is there definitely no way through?"

Crystal pushed the ice with her nose. "It's solid," she said. "We'll have to go back." Her eyes met Rosa's and Rosa felt a sudden flicker of shame that she hadn't listened to Crystal.

"So, this isn't the tunnel we were looking for, Rosa?" called Freya.

"No," Rosa muttered, hating to admit that

she'd been wrong. "We'd better turn round."

Slowly, the unicorns shuffled around. There wasn't much room and Pearl got stuck when she tried turning too fast. Then Matilda got stuck trying to dismount to help her and somehow ended up sitting backwards on Pearl's back, facing her tail! Eventually Matilda managed to right herself, but then she got so muddled directing Pearl where to put her hooves as she turned in the tight space that Violet and Twinkle had to take over, calling out instructions for her. At last everyone was facing the right way, but now Rosa and Crystal were at the back of the group.

"Move over," said Rosa. "Let Crystal get to the front."

But no matter how the unicorns squeezed up, there simply wasn't the room for Crystal to pass, and Freya had to take the lead. Disgruntled, Rosa had to ride at the back until the path opened in to a tiny grotto surrounded by frost-covered rocks. Rosa and Crystal joined the others as they stopped at the edge of a cluster of stalagmites.

"We're lost, aren't we?" Freya said.

Rosa dismounted and opened the map. It was beginning to crease and the edge was torn. "No, we're not," she said, not wanting to admit she didn't have a clue where they were. "We're here." She pointed to a grotto marked on the map.

"I don't think we are, Rosa," said Ariana, looking at the map over her shoulder. "That grotto's bigger than this one and has only one path leading out of it. This one has two."

"First you led us to a dead end and now you say we're in a grotto that's nothing like the one shown on the map," said Freya. "Admit it, Rosa – you don't know where we are."

Rosa's face flushed bright red.

"It's OK," said Ariana quickly. "I think we

might still be able to find the Glittering Cavern. The map shows a pool in the centre of the cavern. It's fed by a stream. Water can't flow up hill. When we leave this grotto, we need to find our way back to the stream we passed earlier and follow the direction it's flowing in. It should lead us to the cavern."

"Luckily I made a list of identifiable things so we can retrace our steps," said Freya. She held up her notebook. "The path we need to get out of here has a stalagmite that's so tall it almost reaches the ceiling."

"I remember seeing that," said Rosa grudgingly.

Freya held out her hand. "Maybe if Ariana and I have the map we might be able to find the cavern."

Rosa held on to the map tightly. She didn't want to hand it over. The adventure had been her idea. She wanted to be the one who found the model of Unicorn Academy and gave it back to Ms Nettles. But there was no getting out of it — she'd got everyone lost, and if she didn't let Freya and Ariana have the map and lead the way, they could be stuck here forever. Rosa shivered. She was sure it was getting colder.

Crystal nudged her. "It's the right thing to do, Rosa," she said, her dark eyes encouraging.

"Fine," Rosa sighed, handing the map over. "You two work out the way then."

CHAPTER SEVEN

With Ariana's excellent map-reading skills, Freya's useful notes and the rest of Diamond dorm chipping in with helpful suggestions, it wasn't too long before the girls and their unicorns arrived at the centre of the maze. As they stepped into the Glittering Cavern, everyone fell silent. They all stared in wonder at the enormous cave. Ice-white stalagmites spiralled upwards to a ceiling embedded with tiny sparkling stalactites as bright and delicate as stars. Water tumbled down a pile of rocks into a glassy pool that shimmered with a blue hue, and icebergs floated across it, looking like giant water lilies.

Matilda's cheeks were turning mauve. "Now what?" she asked, her teeth chattering noisily.

Rosa took in the whole cave. She was convinced that the model was hidden here somewhere, but there were so many nooks and crannies she didn't know where to start her search!

"The model could be anywhere," she said. "Spread out and start looking."

The girls and their unicorns fanned out across the cavern.

"This could take ages," Crystal whispered to Rosa.

And we might not even find it, thought Rosa. The model could be hidden on any of the icy ledges, in one of the crevices, or even on top of one of the massive stalagmites. Rosa began to worry. How would they even see the model if it was on top of a stalagmite, let alone reach it?

She and Crystal searched for ages and Rosa had almost given up hope of ever finding it, when a flicker on the wall caught her eye. "Crystal, what's that over there? I can see something glimmering."

"It looks like a candle," said Crystal. Carefully, she stepped around an ice-covered rock to get a better look.

Suddenly Rosa noticed a hidden arched alcove, dotted with tiny blue crystals, set in the cavern wall. "Look!" Her voice rose in excitement. "There's the model!" Relief flooded through her. Their adventure hadn't been in vain. They'd found the model! Hopefully now everyone would forget she'd got them lost. "Let's get it," she urged.

Crystal took a step closer, but as she did so something shifted under her hooves. She sprang back, almost unseating Rosa. Rosa hung on to Crystal's mane, her heart galloping. She knew she wouldn't hurt herself if she fell off – the island's magic would protect her, catching her in a giant bubble and floating her down to the ground. But island magic wouldn't save Crystal if she fell into the dark pool of water that had opened up centimetres in front of her hooves!

"Rosa! What happened?" asked Violet, riding over on Twinkle.

Rosa stared in surprise as the crack in front of them began to freeze over, concealing the water below. "I've found the model," she said. "It's up there. But it looks like it's been booby-trapped to stop anyone from taking it. If you go too close, the ice cracks."

Jumping from Crystal's back, Rosa selected a large stone from the frosty ground. "Watch this." She threw the stone on to the ground in front of the alcove. A jagged line ran across the ice and it slid apart. With a plop, the stone fell into the dark waters and disappeared.

Freya stared at the crack as the ice froze over

again. "It looks like an enchantment. I've no idea how we can break it, though. We'll have to find a way to reach the model without touching the ice."

"Can that be done?" asked Rosa doubtfully.

"Anything's possible with engineering," said Freya. "If we had materials, we could build a bridge to reach it." She stared at the enchanted ice as if it might give her the solution.

Rosa was just about to suggest they return to the academy in one of Crystal's snow twisters and get some materials to build a bridge, when Freya suddenly spoke. "I've got an idea. It's dangerous, but it should work. It needs all of us to help, though. First I need your hoodies. I'm going to tie them together to make a rope that I'll fix around my waist like a lifeline. Then I'll run across the ice really fast, grab the model and run back. If I'm quick enough, I think I can make it, but if I don't, then you must stop me from sinking by pulling on the rope of hoodies."

Ariana spluttered. "That's much too dangerous. Even if you don't drown, and you probably will, you'll get soaked. And then you'll freeze to death. Let's just go back to school and tell the teachers where the model is."

"But we're here now," said Rosa desperately. After coming this far, she couldn't bear the thought of pulling out and letting the teachers retrieve the model.

"Rosa's right," said Freya. "We can't go back without the model. Not now we're so close."

Rosa's eyes widened in surprise. She wasn't used to Freya agreeing with her!

"I don't mind getting wet," Freya went on, giving Rosa a quick smile. "And I'd like to know if my plan works. Please help us, Ariana."

Ariana shuddered. "I don't know why anyone would want to risk drowning in freezing-cold water, but if you insist on going through with this crazy plan, then I suppose I'll have to help."

"Thanks, Ariana," said Freya. "Hoodies off, everyone, and give them to me."

"No, wait," said Rosa, suddenly remembering. She opened her rucksack. "We don't need to use our hoodies. I brought a rope with me."

"You star!" exclaimed Freya. "That was brilliant thinking!" She lifted her hand and high-fived Rosa. "A rope will be loads better."

"Maybe I should be the one who. . ." Rosa was going to suggest that she went

89

for the model instead of Freya, because she did really want to be the one who picked it up and brought it home, but she broke off as Crystal nudged her hand.

"Team work, remember!" Crystal whispered.

With a rueful sigh, Rosa fell silent. Crystal was right. She loved taking the lead, but maybe some of the others did too and, as they'd already proved, her ideas weren't always the right ones. Rosa suddenly wondered if that was why Ms Rosemary had stopped picking her for things in class. Maybe she was letting the rest of the class have a turn.

She began to tie the rope around Freya's waist, but then Ariana took over because she knew a lot about different types of knots and how secure they were. Once she was happy with how the rope was tied, she handed the end to Honey, who held it firmly between her teeth. Rosa organised everyone else in a line behind the unicorn.

"Ready?" Freya asked, taking up the slack of the rope.

"Ready!" they chorused back.

"Good luck!" shouted Rosa as Freya stepped on to the ice. With a deafening shriek the ice began to split, but Freya ran like the wind, sprinting towards the alcove and snatching the model from the ledge. Black water bubbled up over the sides of the crack as it grew wider. Freya darted back, her plaits flying out behind her and her eyes on the shore as she slipped and slid on the watery ice. The water was rising, sucking her down as it crept up to her ankles. Freya kept on going, arms flailing. She was almost at the shore when the ice gave way completely, tipping her into the murky water with a giant splash. Ariana and Violet both screamed, almost dropping the rope as Freya slipped under the water and out of sight!

CHAPTER EIGHT

Rosa leapt into action as the air filled with alarmed whinnies and yells.

"Pull!" shouted Rosa, her voice rising forcefully above the din. "Everyone pull together. Get behind me and pull, right now! *Pull!*"

She leaned back, straining on the rope till her arms burned. The rope bit into her fingers, but she ignored the pain. The others heaved the rope too. The unicorns joined in, grabbing the rope with their teeth and pulling backwards. As the rope tightened, Rosa, the girls and the unicorns took one giant step back and then another. Rosa gritted her teeth, leaning back and pulling with all her might.

Come on, Freya! Come on! she willed.

Suddenly Freya's arm appeared through the ice.

"Again!" Rosa screamed. "Pull, everyone!"

A second later Freya's head popped up, then the rest of her came with it, flopping on to the ground with icy water pouring from her clothes.

Everyone gathered round while Freya coughed up the water she'd swallowed.

Rosa was full of wonder. "We did it," she exclaimed shakily. "We did it!"

Honey nuzzled up to Freya, breathing on her with her warm breath. The other unicorns did the same, but Freya was shivering badly.

"Wait, I think I can help by using a twister!" said Crystal. "It might warm Freya up." She took a deep breath.

"You can do it," Rosa told her, touching her neck.

Confidence flooded into Crystal's eyes. She stamped a hoof and a mini twister swirled around Freya, hiding her from view. The pink snowflakes worked their magic, warming Freya and drying her soaking clothes. As they faded, Rosa saw that Freya's cheeks were pink again and she had stopped shivering.

"Thank you, Crystal!" Freya smiled.

Rosa hugged Crystal. "Are you OK?" she said, seeing that she was breathing heavily again.

Crystal nodded. "Making twisters is a lot of work, but it's fun!"

Rosa helped Freya to her feet. The girls' eyes met and they hugged.

"Thanks," Freya whispered in Rosa's ear. "I heard you shouting and telling everyone what to do. If you hadn't done that . . ." Her voice trailed off.

"I'm just glad you're all right," said Rosa, feeling a warm glow spread through her from her head to her toes. Maybe she and Freya could be friends after all – really good friends. Suddenly she remembered something. "The model!"

"What? This, you mean?" Freya grinned and

opened her right hand. The model of the academy was nestling safely in her palm. The unicorns whinnied and the girls whooped. "There was no way I was going to drop it," said Freya, inspecting it. "It's a beautiful piece of engineering. Look at how the doors and windows all open."

"Even better — it can get us back to school!" said Rosa.

"How does it work?" asked Matilda.

"I think we just tell it where we want to go," said Rosa. As she spoke the model started to glow.

Freya pushed the model into Rosa's hand. "Go on. You do it. You had the idea for coming on this adventure. You should be the one to take us home." Everyone else nodded and Rosa felt her heart swell with happiness as she looked around at Diamond dorm, all united for once.

Crystal nuzzled Rosa's cheek. "I'm so glad I'm paired with you."

Rosa hugged her. "That makes two of us. I wouldn't want any other unicorn but you. Now let's go home." She raised her voice. "Unicorn Academy!" she shouted. A fierce wind suddenly swirled around the cavern, whipping the girls' hair behind them. A second later they and their unicorns were all swept into the air and then Rosa's eyes blurred. With a chorus of squeals and whinnies, the girls and their unicorns were whisked away.

★

Bump! Rosa landed on her bottom. *I'm sitting on grass*, she realised as the wind faded away and she saw they were on the lawn directly outside Ms Nettles' study. As they all scrambled up, Ms Nettles and pretty Ms Willow, the school nurse, ran out through the tall glass doors.

"Girls, what is the meaning of this behaviour?" Ms Nettles exclaimed.

"Ms Nettles, I. . ." Rosa began then, catching Crystal's eye, she grinned sheepishly. "Sorry, I mean *we* – all the girls in Diamond dorm – heard that the magic map was broken because the Unicorn Academy model was missing, so we thought we'd try and find it."

Rosa continued the story, inviting her dorm-mates to chip in, while Ms Nettles listened in silence. When they reached the end, Rosa handed the tiny model of the school to Ms Nettles and Freya gave her the map.

"Well," said Ms Nettles, her glasses rattling on the end of her bony nose, "I really ought to be cross with you for breaking so many rules. Let me see," she listed them off on her fingers. "There was entering Ms Primrose's study, which is out of bounds, taking the map, not to mention going out of school without permission."

Ms Willow tutted in concern. "Girls, you have been very bad, brave but bad. Both you and your unicorns could have been hurt. I can see Ms Nettles and I are going to have to keep a careful eye on you!" She tucked a stray blonde curl behind her ear. "Ms Nettles, they all look frozen. May I go and sort them out some mugs of hot chocolate?"

Ms Nettles smiled. "I think that would be an excellent idea, Ms Willow. Girls, don't think that I'm not grateful," she continued as Ms Willow hurried away. "The magical map will most definitely work now it is complete again. But Ms Willow is right – I shall be watching you all *very* closely in future." Her lips twitched as if she was trying not to smile. "No more dangerous adventures from now on, at least not without asking my permission first. Now, off you go. Take your unicorns back to the stables. Rosa, nice team work today. And well done for bonding with Crystal."

"Thank you, Ms Nettles. . . Wait, have we bonded?" As Rosa turned her head to look at Crystal a shimmer of purple caught her eye. She grabbed at the lock of hair, the exact same colour as Crystal's mane, and stared at it in wonder.

"Crystal, we *have* bonded!" Rosa threw her arms around Crystal.

Ms Nettles finally stepped in and shooed everyone back to the stables.

Rosa and her friends settled the unicorns with a huge feast of sky berries.

"You look tired," said Rosa, stroking Crystal's neck.

"I am tired," said Crystal happily. "But this has been my best day at Unicorn Academy so far. My magic is brilliant, but the best thing was bonding with you, Rosa. You're my best friend ever."

Crystal stamped her hoof, sending a whirl of pink sparkles into the air. A flurry of snow feil, landing on Rosa and Crystal in a frosty white heart shape.

"Aw," said Rosa, with a giggle. "You're my best friend too." She dropped a kiss on Crystal's nose. We make a great team."

Rosa gave Crystal one last hug then she ran after her friends back to Diamond dorm, where steaming mugs of hot chocolate topped with swirly cream, chocolate sprinkles and marshmallows were waiting for them.

"I know, let's have a feast!" said Matilda. "I've got biscuits somewhere." She dived into her wardrobe and began pulling out jumpers and odd socks.

"I've got cupcakes," said Rosa, making for her wardrobe.

"I've got a bar of chocolate," said Violet.

"Toffee popcorn, anyone?" called Ariana, producing an extra-large bag.

"And I've got a box of chocolate spanners," said Freya, shyly producing a long box.

"To the girls in Diamond dorm and our unicorns," said Rosa, holding up a mug of hot chocolate. "Here's to our next exciting adventure."

The girls chinked their mugs together. "To our next exciting adventure!"

Another MAGICAL series from Nosy Crow!

SNOW SiSTERS

SNOW SiSTERS
ASTRID FOSS
THE SILVER SECRET
nosy crow

SNOW SiSTERS
ASTRID FOSS
THE CRYSTAL ROSE
nosy crow

SNOW SiSTERS
ASTRID FOSS
THE FROZEN RAINBOW
nosy crow

SNOW SiSTERS
ASTRID FOSS
THE ENCHANTED WATERFALL
nosy crow

PRINCESS of PETS

Look out for a BRILLIANT new
Nosy Crow series from the author
of The Rescue Princesses!

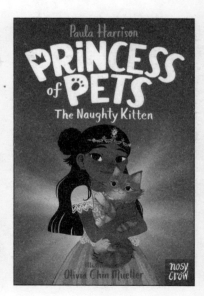

Animal adventures,
friendship and a royal family!